A Note to Parents and Caregivers:

Read-it! Readers are for children who are just starting on the amazing road to reading. These beautiful books support both the acquisition of reading skills and the love of books.

 The PURPLE LEVEL presents basic topics and objects using high frequency words and simple language patterns.

 The RED LEVEL presents familiar topics using common words and repeating sentence patterns.

 The BLUE LEVEL presents new ideas using a larger vocabulary and varied sentence structure.

 The YELLOW LEVEL presents more challenging ideas, a broad vocabulary, and wide variety in sentence structure.

 The GREEN LEVEL presents more complex ideas, an extended vocabulary range, and expanded language structures.

 The ORANGE LEVEL presents a wide range of ideas and concepts using challenging vocabulary and complex language structures.

When sharing a book with your child, read in short stretches, pausing often to talk about the pictures. Have your child turn the pages and point to the pictures and familiar words. And be sure to reread favorite stories or parts of stories.

There is no right or wrong way to share books with children. Find time to read with your child, and pass on the legacy of literacy.

Adria F. Klein, Ph.D.
Professor Emeritus
California State University
San Bernardino, California

To my good friend Jennifer Lee Mundee, and her little dog Ragamuffin

First American edition published in 2005 by
Picture Window Books
5115 Excelsior Boulevard
Suite 232
Minneapolis, MN 55416
877-845-8392
www.picturewindowbooks.com

First published in Canada in 1999 by
Les éditions Héritage inc.
300 Arran Street, Saint Lambert
Quebec, Canada J4R 1K5

Printed in the United States of America.

Library of Congress Cataloging-in-Publication Data
Sarrazin, Marisol, 1965–
Peppy, Patch, and the bath / written and illustrated by Marisol Sarrazin.
p. cm. — (Read-it! readers)
Summary: Patch the puppy's grandfather, Peppy, instructs him in the best canine techniques for bathing.
ISBN 1-4048-1032-3 (hardcover)
[1. Dogs—Fiction. 2. Animals—Infancy—Fiction. 3. Grandfathers—Fiction. 4. Baths—Fiction. 5. Stories in rhyme—Fiction.] I. Title. II. Series.

PZ8.3.S2358Pab 2004
[E]—dc22   2004023915

Peppy, Patch, and the Bath

Read-it! Readers
Green Level

Written and Illustrated by
Marisol Sarrazin

Special thanks to our advisers for their expertise:

Adria F. Klein, Ph.D.
Professor Emeritus, California State University
San Bernardino, California

Susan Kesselring, M.A.
Literacy Educator
Rosemount - Apple Valley - Eagan (Minnesota) School District

PICTURE WINDOW BOOKS
Minneapolis, Minnesota

Hi! My name is Patch. And this
is Thomas, my master.

4

That's Peppy. I call him Mr. Know-It-All.
He's also my grandpa. He's teaching me
all the things that a little dog should know.

One day, my grandpa decided to teach me how to smell good.

He scratched his nose and began to speak.

"Patch, little Patch, keep this in your head:
A puppy dog shouldn't smell like a hog,
and certainly not if he's well bred.

But real dogs don't take showers.
No! What you need is a bath,
both morning and night.
Grandpa Peppy will teach you to do it right.

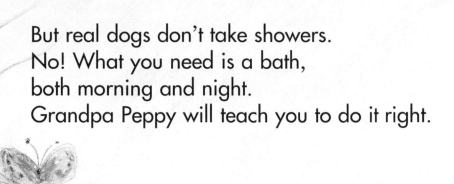

You have to give the water a chance.
Jump right in and make it dance!

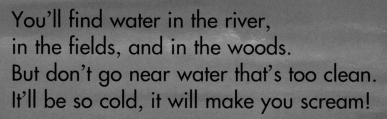

You'll find water in the river,
in the fields, and in the woods.
But don't go near water that's too clean.
It'll be so cold, it will make you scream!

13

Go ahead: stick in your paw,
your belly, your chest, all the way to your jaw.

Wade in with your front paws
and back paws, too.
Get used to the water! It's good for you!

15

When it's nice and muddy, jump right in,
splash around, and go for a swim.
Take life easy. Stay all day!
Dive to the bottom—that's Peppy's way to play!

Once you're soaked like an old washcloth,
there's no use getting dried off.
Go for a run on the beach.
The sand is warm, and it's easy to reach.

18

With all that water you've got in your coat,
you could fill up a sandcastle's moat.
Or I'll bet those picnickers would like to play.
A wet, shaking dog will brighten their day!

Then go exploring like a brave little dog—
dig up a jewel from under a log.

There are so many wonders on the forest floor.
I'm sure you'll find two or three, maybe more.

23

Mushrooms, thistles, and ferns abound—
all of them prizes for a hunting hound.
Burrs and cattails stuck in your coat,
and the taste of pond water in your throat.

25

Then search out the sweetest perfume.
Stick to it like dust to a broom.
From tip to toe you'll be covered,

and from top to bottom you'll be smothered
in the finest scent known to dogs.

This black-and-white friend smells so fine.
Just sneak up on him from behind.

Surprise him, and he'll share his cologne.
Thomas will be thrilled when you get home.

Tomato juice is the only cure—
that's what Thomas thinks, for sure—

but that's a different kind of bath!"

More *Read-it!* Readers

Bright pictures and fun stories help you practice your
reading skills. Look for more books at your level.

Alex and the Team Jersey by Gilles Tibo
Alex and Toolie by Gilles Tibo
Clever Cat by Karen Wallace
Felicio's Incredible Invention by Mireille Villeneuve
Flora McQuack by Penny Dolan
Izzie's Idea by Jillian Powell
Mysteries for Felicio by Mireille Villeneuve
Naughty Nancy by Anne Cassidy
Parents Do the Weirdest Things! by Louise Tondreau-Levert
Peppy, Patch, and the Bath by Marisol Sarrazin
Peppy, Patch, and the Postman by Marisol Sarrazin
Peppy, Patch, and the Socks by Marisol Sarrazin
The Princess and the Frog by Margaret Nash
The Roly-Poly Rice Ball by Penny Dolan
Run! by Sue Ferraby
Sausages! by Anne Adeney
Stickers, Shells, and Snow Globes by Dana Meachen Rau
Theodore the Millipede by Carole Tremblay
The Truth About Hansel and Gretel by Karina Law
Willie the Whale by Joy Oades

Looking for a specific title or level? A complete list
of *Read-it!* Readers is available on our Web site:
www.picturewindowbooks.com